My Weirdel

Mrs. Bacon Is Fakin'!

Dan Gutman

Pictures by
Jim Paillot

HARPER

An Imprint of HarperCollinsPublishers

To music teachers, musicians,
and music lovers everywhere

Thanks to Rachel DiPilla,
Steve DiPilla, Jane Canter,
Eric DiVito, and Linda Mirabella

My Weirder-est School #6: Mrs. Bacon Is Fakin'!
Text copyright © 2020 by Dan Gutman
Illustrations copyright © 2020 by Jim Paillot
All rights reserved. Printed in the United States of America.
No part of this book may be used or reproduced in any manner whatsoever without
written permission except in the case of brief quotations embodied in critical articles
and reviews. For information address HarperCollins Children's Books, a division of
HarperCollins Publishers, 195 Broadway, New York, NY 10007.
www.harpercollinschildrens.com

ISBN 978-0-06-269116-3 (pbk bdg.) — ISBN 978-0-06-269117-0 (library bdg.)

Typography by Laura Mock
20 21 22 23 24   PC/BRR   10 9 8 7 6 5 4 3 2 1
❖
First Edition

Contents

Ridorkulous!

My name is A.J. and I know what you're thinking. You're thinking that "ridorkulous" isn't a word. Well, that's where you're *wrong*! Ridorkulous is something that's ridiculous and makes you look like a dork.

I ought to know ridorkulous is a word

because I invented it! Something totally ridorkulous happened at Ella Mentry School recently. We had just finished pledging the allegiance in Mr. Cooper's class.

"Turn to page twenty-three in your math books," he said.

Ugh, I hate math.

That's when the weirdest thing in the history of the world happened. Our principal, Mr. Klutz, ran into the room. He has no hair at all. When Mr. Klutz gets mad, he can't tear his hair out because he doesn't have any.

He was out of breath and panting. That means he was wearing pants. Mr. Klutz was also wearing binoculars around his neck.

"Follow me!" he shouted. Then he ran out the door.

"Not again," muttered Mr. Cooper.

We all ran after Mr. Klutz.

"Maybe it's a fire drill," said Andrea, this annoying girl with curly brown hair.

"Maybe it's a lockdown," said Michael, who never ties his shoes.

"Maybe the aliens have landed," said Ryan, who will eat anything, even stuff that isn't food.

"It must be important if we have to evacuate," said Alexia, this girl who rides a skateboard all the time.

"Evacuate?" I said. "I just *went* to the bathroom."

"Evacuate means to leave, dumbhead," Andrea told me.

I was going to say something mean to Andrea, but I couldn't think of anything. I didn't really care *why* we had to leave the building. As long as we were getting out of math.

Mr. Klutz led us to the playground.

"Look!" he shouted, pointing at the monkey bars.

And you'll never believe what we saw out there.

A goose.

There were two of them, actually. Two

gooses. I mean geese. For more than one goose, you're supposed to say geese. Nobody knows why. A female goose is called a goose, but a male goose is called a gander, which makes no sense at all. I know stuff like that because I'm in the gifted and talented program.

So we took a gander at the geese.

"They're Canadian geese," said Mr. Klutz, peering through his binoculars.

"How do you know?" asked Andrea.

"He checked their driver's licenses," I said. Nobody laughed, even though the idea of a goose driving a car was hilarious.

"A Canadian goose has a black head and a white mark on its chin," explained Mr. Klutz.

"They're adorable!" said Emily, Andrea's crybaby friend.

"What's that annoying noise?" asked Neil, who we call the nude kid even though he wears clothes.

Neil was right. The geese were making a horrible honking sound.

"That's their mating call," said Mr. Klutz. "When geese mate, they stay together for the rest of their lives."

"Isn't that romantic?" said Andrea. "The geese are in *love*!"

Ugh. Andrea said the L word. Disgusting!

"Awwwwww," said all the girls.

"Ewwwwww," said all the boys.

The geese kept honking at each other. It was annoying. I covered my ears to block out the sound.

"Can we chase them?" I suggested.

"That's not nice, Arlo!" said Andrea, who calls me by my real name because she knows I don't like it. "Animals are our friends. You shouldn't hurt animals just because you don't like their mating call. We should cherish *all* living creatures."

Why can't a truck full of geese fall on Andrea's head?

She's ridorkulous.*

---

*What's the difference between a piano and a fish?
You can't tuna fish.

The Petting Zoo

After a few minutes of staring at the geese, we went back to class.

"Turn to page twenty-three in your math books," said Mr. Cooper.

That's when an announcement came over the loudspeaker: "MR. COOPER'S CLASS, PLEASE REPORT TO ROOM 303."

Yay! No math!

Mr. Cooper slammed his math book closed.

"Room 303?" asked Ryan. "What's room 303?"

"I never heard of room 303," said Andrea, Little Miss Know-It-All.

"Me neither," said Emily, who's only heard of stuff that Andrea has heard of.

We lined up like Pringles and walked a million hundred miles to room 303. A sign over the door said BAND ROOM.

Oh, yeah! The band room. That's where they keep musical instruments. We've never been in there. Only the upper grades get to play instruments.

We looked around. The room was filled with drums and trumpets and saxophones and lots of other stuff you hit or blow into. And you'll never believe who walked into the door at that moment.

Nobody! It would hurt if you walked into a door. But you'll never believe who walked into the door*way*.

It was our music teacher, Mr. Loring.* He teaches us how to sing weird songs like "Row, Row, Row Your Boat." Mr. Loring is boring. He handed out name tags for us to wear.

---

*Knock, knock!
Who's there?
Little old lady.
Little old lady who?
I didn't know you could yodel.

"Are you the band teacher too?" asked Andrea.

"No," said Mr. Loring. "I'm the band aide."

We all giggled because Mr. Loring said he was a Band-Aid.

"I'm here to introduce you to Mrs. Bacon," said Mr. Loring. "Before she became the school band teacher, she was a conductor."

"She drove trains?" I asked.

"Not *that* kind of conductor, dumbhead!" said Andrea.

I was going to say something mean to Andrea, but I didn't have the chance because you'll never believe who poked her head into the door at that moment.

Nobody! Why would anybody poke her head into a door? Didn't we just go over that a few paragraphs ago? But you'll never believe who poked her head into the door*way*.

It was Mrs. Bacon, of course. Who *else* could it be? Her name is right on the cover of the book!

Mrs. Bacon was wearing an army uniform and holding a chopstick in her hand. We all clapped, which is what you do whenever somebody gets introduced.

"Why do you think Mrs. Bacon has a chopstick in her hand?" Michael whispered to me.

"Maybe she's going out for Chinese food after this," I whispered back.

"Thank you," said Mrs. Bacon. "I *love* music. I feel the passion of music in my soul. Playing music can heal the sick. It

can end wars. Music can bring people together. It can change the world."

"*Everybody* loves music!" said Andrea. What a brownnoser.

"That's right!" said Mrs. Bacon. "Music is the universal language."

"Does that mean they have music on other planets of the universe?" I asked.

"It wouldn't surprise me!" said Mrs. Bacon.

"Is there music on Uranus?" I asked.

Everybody laughed because I said "Uranus." Any time you want to get your friends to laugh, just mention Uranus. That's the first rule of being a kid.

Everybody laughed except Andrea, of *course*. She just rolled her eyes. Then she started waving her hand around like she was trying to signal a plane from a desert island. Mrs. Bacon called on her.

"I already know how to play an instrument," said Andrea. "I take violin lessons after school."

"That's *wonderful*, Andrea!" said Mrs. Bacon.

Andrea takes lessons in *everything* after school. If they gave a class in toenail clipping, she would take that class so she could get better at it.

"I thought you didn't approve of violins," I told Andrea.

"Not violins, Arlo!" she said. "It's *violence* that I don't like."

I know the difference between violins

and violence. I was just yanking Andrea's chain. But those words sound way too much alike.

"Welcome to my musical petting zoo," said Mrs. Bacon. "As third graders, you can learn how to play an instrument this year. And when you reach fourth grade, you may get to play in the school orchestra. Isn't that exciting?"

"Yes!" shouted all the girls.

"No!" shouted all the boys.

School orchestra? They should call it the "dorkestra."

Mrs. Bacon showed us a bunch of instruments and talked about each one. Did you know the saxophone was invented by a guy named Adolphe Sax? It's true! I guess the trumpet was invented by Donald Trump.

"Go ahead, try the instruments," said Mrs. Bacon. "That's why I call it a petting zoo."

We picked up instruments and started fooling around with them. Ryan tried a big bass drum. Emily tried a flute. Neil tried something called a glockenspiel. It was weird.

"Do you know how to play all these instruments, Mrs. Bacon?" asked Andrea.

"Of course," she replied.

"No way she can play *all* the instruments," I whispered to Michael. "I bet she can't play *any* of them."

"Yeah, I say Mrs. Bacon is fakin'!" he whispered back.

"Maybe she isn't a band teacher at all," I whispered. "Did you ever think of that? Maybe she kidnapped the *real* band teacher."

"I heard that!" said Mrs. Bacon.

Uh-oh.

"Would you like me to prove that I can play these instruments?" she asked.

"Yes!" we shouted.

Mrs. Bacon picked up a drum and strapped it to her back. Then she attached a string to her foot so that when she moved it, a mallet hit the drum. Then she wrapped a metal thing around her neck that had a harmonica, a kazoo, and a trumpet sticking out of it, right in front of her face. Then she put a cymbal on top of her head. Then she attached a tambourine to one knee. Finally, she picked up a violin.

That's when the weirdest thing in the history of the world happened. Mrs. Bacon played "Twinkle, Twinkle, Little Star" using all those instruments at the same time! It was amazing!

"WOW," we said, which is "MOM" upside down.

I guess she *can* play all those instruments. But Mrs. Bacon is weird.

Band Karate

We fooled around with the instruments for a long time. We all sounded pretty horrible, except for Andrea of course. Mrs. Bacon told us not to get discouraged. She said it takes hard work and lots of practice to get good. She also told us our parents could rent an instrument for us and then come see us play at a recital.

"Okay, it's time to choose your instrument," Mrs. Bacon announced. "What do you want to play?"

"Clarinet!" shouted Andrea. "It's the only instrument here that I don't already know how to play."

"Flute!" shouted Emily. "It will be easy to carry home from school."

"Trumpet!" shouted Michael. "Because they play them in the army."

"I want to play French horn," said Ryan, "because I like French fries."

"Drums!" shouted Neil. "Banging on stuff is fun."

"I want to play trombone," said Alexia,

"because that slide thing is cool."

"How about you, A.J.?" asked Mrs. Bacon. "Which instrument do *you* want to play?"

"I don't want to play *any* instrument."

You could have heard a pin drop.

Well, that is if anybody had pins with them. But why would you bring pins to school?

Everybody was staring at me. It was like the earth had stopped turning.

"I beg your pardon?" asked Mrs. Bacon.

That's grown-up talk for "What?" Grown-ups are always begging to be pardoned. Nobody knows why.

"I said I don't want to play *any*

instrument," I told her. "I just like to play video games."

Mrs. Bacon dropped to the floor like an elephant had just fallen on her head.

"Noooooooooo!" she screamed.

She got down on her knees in front of me. Tears were running down her cheeks. Either she's *really* emotional, or Mrs. Bacon is fakin'.

"*Anyone* can click a button on a video game," she moaned. "It takes *effort* to make beautiful music. I think video games are bad for kids."

"But they're *fun*," I said.

"Playing music is fun too," said Mrs. Bacon. "Won't you just *try* an instrument, A.J.? You might become the next Beethoven!"

"Who's that?" I asked.

"Arlo," said Andrea, "Beethoven was the greatest composer who ever lived!"

"You might be the next Mozart!" said Mrs. Bacon.*

"Never heard of her," I replied.

---

*What is Mozart doing right now?
Decomposing.

"Mozart was a *man*, dumbhead," said Andrea.

"Oh, snap!" said Ryan.

"What a waste it would be to have musical talent and not use it," said Mrs. Bacon. "A.J., you might be the next Tchaikovsky, the next Rachmaninoff, the next Shostakovich!"

She named a bunch of other people with names I couldn't pronounce.

"Playing an instrument is boring," I replied. "I don't want to spend hours practicing some dumb instrument when I could be playing video games or doing something fun, like going to karate."

When I said "karate," Mrs. Bacon's eyes lit up.

Well, not really. It would be dangerous if your eyes lit up. Your whole head might catch on fire!

"A.J., have you ever heard of band karate?" Mrs. Bacon asked.

"NO," I said, which is "ON" backward.

"In band karate, you earn colored belts

as you get better at your instrument," said Mrs. Bacon.

"I'm listening," I said.

"It's sort of like regular karate, except you don't kick or punch anybody," explained Mrs. Bacon. "As you practice hard and learn new songs, you earn points. You start with a white belt, and then you move on to your yellow, orange, green, blue, purple, brown, and red belt. Finally, if you practice enough, you could earn a black belt."

Hmmm. Winning stuff is cool.

"Oh, I forgot to mention," said Mrs. Bacon, "while you're with me in the band room, you may have to miss some of your regular classes."

WHAT!?

"You mean, like math?" I asked.

"Yes," said Mrs. Bacon. "Band members may have to miss some math classes."

"I'm in!" I shouted.

"Hooray!" said Mrs. Bacon. She jumped up and high-fived me. Then she gave me a hug.

Ugh. No hugs! Hugging is gross. It's almost as bad as kissing, but not quite.

Most of the instruments had already been taken by the other kids. But on the floor in the corner of the room was a big twisty gold horn.

"What's that?" I asked.

"That's a tuba," said Mrs. Bacon.

"A tube of what?" I asked.

"No, dumbhead," said Andrea. "It's *called* a tuba."

I was going to say something mean to Andrea, but I decided to pick up the tuba instead. It was *really* heavy. But it looked cool.

"How do you play this thing?" I asked.

"You blow into the mouthpiece," said Mrs. Bacon.

I blew into the mouthpiece. It made a funny sound.

"Dude," said Ryan, "that sounds like an elephant farted."

Everybody laughed. Making elephant

fart noises is cool.

"That's good enough for me," I said. "I'll play the tuba."

Maybe playing an instrument wouldn't be so bad after all.

Every Good Burger Deserves Fries

We only meet with Mrs. Bacon once a week. The next Thursday, before going into school, I went out to the playground to see if the geese were still there. Not only were they still there, but now there were *four* of them. They were squawking and honking at each other. I guess this is their mating season.

The bell rang, and I made it to Mr. Cooper's class just in time to pledge the allegiance.

"Turn to page twenty-three in your math books," said Mr. Cooper.

"Sorry," I told him. "We have to go to room 303."

We all got up and went to room 303.

"We get our instruments today!" Neil said when we got there. "I can't wait to get my drum."

"I'm so excited!" Andrea said.

"Me too!" said Emily, who's always excited when Andrea is excited.

Mrs. Bacon was waiting for us at the door.*

---

*How do you make a bandstand?
Take away their chairs.

"Oh, you're not ready to play instruments yet," she told us. "Today, we're going to learn how to read music."

What?! I hate reading. Reading is boring. I don't even know why you're reading this book.

"I already *know* how to read music," said Andrea, who loves letting everybody know that she knows stuff nobody else knows. "I've been playing violin for three years."

"Don't you get tired?" I asked.

Mrs. Bacon went to the board and drew five lines and a funny-looking squiggle.

"Each line represents a different musical note," she told us. "E, G, B, D, and F.

They're easy to remember. Just think of Every Good Burger Deserves Fries. Or Elvis's Guitar Broke Down Friday. Or Empty Garbage Before Dad Flips. Or . . ."

She went on like that for a while.

"Each space represents a different note too," continued Mrs. Bacon. "F, A, C, and E. Just think of the word 'face.'"

I didn't get it. One of the lines was the note F and one of the spaces was also the note F. How can there be two Fs? This was starting to get confusing. Then Mrs. Bacon drew five more lines below the first five lines, and another funny-looking squiggle.

"Let's move down to the bass clef," she said. "The lines here are G, B, D, F, and A. You can remember that by saying Good Burritos Don't Fall Apart, or Great Big Dogs Fight Animals. The spaces here are A, C, E, and G. You can remember *that* by saying All Cows Eat Grass."

Huh? What's a clef? Playing video games is a lot easier than learning how to read music.

"This is called a rest," Mrs. Bacon said, drawing a squiggly thing on the board. "It means you take a little rest between notes."

"I'm not tired," I said. "What if I don't want to take a rest?"

Andrea rolled her eyes.

"Let's talk about notes," said Mrs. Bacon, drawing on the board. "This is a half note. There are whole notes, half notes, quarter notes, and blah blah blah blah . . ."

By this time, I was totally confused. I started pretending my pencil was a rocket ship flying across my desk. Any time you're bored at school, just pretend your pencil is a rocket ship. That's the first rule of being a kid.

"I don't get it," I said. "Why would I want to play half a note? I say if you're going to play a note, you should play the *whole* note. My parents always tell me if you're going to do something, you should do it right."

"This is going to be harder than I thought," mumbled Mrs. Bacon.

I looked over at Michael. He was staring out the window.

"Two half notes equal one whole note blah blah," said Mrs. Bacon. "And four quarter notes equal one blah blah. A whole note is four beats. A beat is blah blah a half note is two blah blah a quarter note is one blah blah an eighth note is a half a blah blah blah . . ."

What a snoozefest. I had no idea what she was talking about.

Then it hit me. To play music, you've got to do reading and math! It wasn't fair! The only reason I agreed to learn the tuba was to get out of reading and math!

I looked around. Ryan had stuck two pencils in his nostrils and was pretending to be a walrus. Neil crumpled up a piece of paper and was trying to balance it on his head.

Mrs. Bacon took a tissue and wiped her forehead with it. Grown-ups are always sweating even when it's not hot.

"Our time is up for today," she said. "I'll see you next Thursday."

The Greatest Song in the World

The next Thursday I got to school early, so I went around to the playground to look at the geese. And you'll never believe what I saw out there.

More geese! There were *eight* of them. It was creepy. Where were all these geese coming from? Canada, I guess.

The bell rang, and I went inside the school. That's when the weirdest thing in the history of the world happened. All the grown-ups were wearing earmuffs!

Mrs. Roopy, our librarian, was wearing

earmuffs. Mr. Docker, our science teacher, was wearing earmuffs. Mrs. Cooney, our nurse, was wearing earmuffs.

"Why are you wearing earmuffs?" I asked Mrs. Cooney.

"Uh, I'm chilly," she replied.

When I got to class, an announcement came over the loudspeaker: "THIRD GRADERS CAN PICK UP THEIR INSTRU-MENTS TODAY IN THE BAND ROOM. AND TEACHERS WHO WOULD LIKE TO PURCHASE NOISE-CANCELING HEAD-PHONES CAN GET THEM IN THE FRONT OFFICE."

After we pledged the allegiance, we went to room 303. Our instruments were lined up waiting for us. Ryan got his French horn. Michael got his trumpet. Andrea got her clarinet. Emily got her flute. Alexia got her trombone. Neil got his drum. I got my tuba. It was cool.*

"Are we going to learn more about reading music today?" asked Andrea.

"No," said Mrs. Bacon. "I think reading music is a little bit advanced for some students. Our first recital is in three weeks. So

---

*How do you fix a broken tuba?
With a tuba glue.

I've decided to teach you how to play by ear."

WHAT?! How was I supposed to play a tuba with my ears?

"Can't I use my mouth instead?" I asked.

Everybody laughed even though I didn't say anything funny.

Mrs. Bacon told us to take the mouth-piece off our instrument so we could learn how to blow into it the right way. She showed each of us how to do it.

"Now blow," she said.

We blew into our mouthpieces. It was an awful sound.

"Cheeks and leaks make squeaks," said Mrs. Bacon. "Try again."

It was still pretty horrible, but a little better. We did it a few more times. After we started getting the hang of it, Mrs. Bacon said it was time to try our first song. We put the mouthpieces back on our instruments.

"This is one of my favorites," Mrs. Bacon said, getting some paper out of her desk. "It's called 'Hot Cross Buns.' I'm going to pass out—"

"She's gonna pass out!" shouted Ryan.

"Call an ambulance!" I shouted.

"I'm going to pass out a piece of paper to each of you," said Mrs. Bacon.

Oh. The paper had the words to "Hot Cross Buns" on it. It goes like this . . .

Hot cross buns!
Hot cross buns!
One a penny, two a penny,
Hot cross buns!

What a ridorkulous song. Why would anybody make a song about buns? And you're not going to make much money if you sell buns for a penny. The buns must be pretty yucky if you can get them so cheap.

We all picked up our instruments. Mrs. Bacon showed each of us how to play "Hot Cross Buns."

"It's easy," she said. "There are only three notes in the whole song."

What?! How can a song only have three notes?

"Let's try it," said Mrs. Bacon. "Ready? One . . . two . . . three . . ."

She waved her chopstick around and we all tried to play the three notes.

It was awful.

"No! No!" shouted Mrs. Bacon, holding her ears. "Try again."

She waved her chopstick again and we all played. It was horrible.

"No! No!" shouted Mrs. Bacon. "You're not getting it! I want you to *feel* the hot cross buns! Try again."

She waved her chopstick and we played. It was terrible.

"No!" Mrs. Bacon yelled. "You sound like those geese out in the playground!"

She was right. We did sound a little like honking geese.

"I think I'm getting a headache," said Mrs. Bacon. "Take five, everybody."

"Five *what*?" I asked.

"That means take a five-minute break, dumbhead," Andrea told me.

Mrs. Bacon went to get aspirin. I was going to say something mean to Andrea, but instead I did what I always do when the teacher leaves the room. I climbed up on my desk and shook my butt at the class.

"Stop fooling around, Arlo!" said Andrea. "You'll get in troub—"

Andrea didn't have the chance to finish her sentence because Michael snuck up behind her and blasted his trumpet right in her ear! Andrea freaked out and fell off her chair. It was hilarious.

And you'll never believe who walked into the room at that moment.

It was Mr. Klutz!

I climbed down from my desk. That's when Mrs. Bacon came back into the room.

"Mr. Klutz!" she said. "To what do we owe the pleasure of your company?"

That's grown-up talk for "What are *you* doing here?"

"Oh, I just wanted to see how the students were making out with their instruments," Mr. Klutz replied.

"Gross!" we all shouted. "We're not making out with our instruments!"

Mr. Klutz walked over to me.

"Ah, yes," he said. "This brings back memories. I played the tuba once, you know."

"Just once?" I asked. "I guess you weren't very good."

Mr. Klutz told us he played the tuba in his college marching band. For fun, he said, he would stick his head in the tuba and have his friends blow into it. It made a funny sound because his bald head made a tight seal against the horn.

"Can you show us?" asked Ryan.

"Sure!" said Mr. Klutz. "Watch this."

He stuck his head inside my tuba.

"Okay," Mr. Klutz said. "Blow!"

I blew into my tuba. It made a hilarious

sound. Everybody laughed, even Mrs. Bacon.

"Wait a minute," said Mr. Klutz. "I think my head may be stuck."

It was true. I guess his head was bigger than it was during his college days.

"Mr. Klutz's head is stuck in the tuba!" shouted Neil.

"Help!" shouted Mr. Klutz. "Get me out of here!"

Everybody rushed over to help.

And you'll never believe who walked into the room at that moment.

It was Dr. Carbles, the president of the Board of Education!

"Klutz!" he shouted. "Get your head out

of that tuba! What's the meaning of this?"

I was going to give Dr. Carbles a dictionary so he could look up the meaning
of "this." But that's when Mr. Klutz yanked
his head out of the tuba.

"Ouch!" he shouted. "I was just showing the students—"

But he didn't have the chance to finish his sentence.

"I'm not paying you to stick your head into a tuba, Klutz!" thundered Dr. Carbles.

"But . . . but . . . but . . ." said Mr. Klutz.

We all giggled because Mr. Klutz said "but," which sounds just like "butt" but only has one *T*.

"And you!" shouted Dr. Carbles as he pointed at Mrs. Bacon. "I'm not paying you to wave a stick around while these kids make horrible honking noises! I'll be at your recital in three weeks. If it's as bad as this, you'll be fired!"

Musicians Are Gross

"Let's talk about spit," Mrs. Bacon said as we took our seats the next Thursday.

Well, *that's* a weird way to start class.

Mrs. Bacon told us that when you blow into a mouthpiece, some of your saliva gets inside it. She said that brass instruments like trumpets, trombones, and tubas have this thing called a "spit valve." Every so often you need to open it to blow the spit out of your instrument.

Mrs. Bacon took Alexia's trombone and showed her the spit valve. Then she told us to find the spit valve on our instruments. I looked all over my tuba until I found the spit valve. I pushed it, and some spit dripped out.

"Hey, look!" I announced. "My tuba is peeing!"

Everybody thought that was hilarious. Well, everybody except Andrea, of course.

"That's disgusting, Arlo," she said. "Why don't you take your tuba to the boys' room and empty your spit there?"

Hmmm, not a bad idea. Going to the bathroom is a great way to get out of class. That's the first rule of being a kid.*

"Can I go to the bathroom?" I asked Mrs. Bacon.

"I *hope* so," she replied. "If you can't, you should go to a doctor."

Oh, yeah, I always forget. Grown-ups don't like it when you say *can* I go to the

_____

*I keep hearing music coming out of my computer printer. I think the paper is jamming.

bathroom. Nobody knows why. We're supposed to say *may* I go to the bathroom.

"*May I* go to the bathroom?" I asked.

"Certainly," replied Mrs. Bacon.

I walked down the hall to the boys'
room. It wasn't easy getting into the stall
with my tuba. But I did it.

I found the spit valve and opened it.
Then I blew into the mouthpiece.

That's when the weirdest thing in the
history of the world happened.

MY MOUTHPIECE FELL INTO THE
TOILET BOWL!

Noooooooooo!

I thought I was gonna die! This was
the worst thing to happen since National

Poetry Month! I wanted to run away to Antarctica and live with the penguins.

I didn't know what to say. I didn't know what to do. I had to think fast. So I ran back to room 303.

"I need your help," I whispered to Ryan. "I dropped my tuba mouthpiece into the toilet bowl."

"Dude, I'm not sticking my hand into a toilet bowl," Ryan replied.

"Me neither!" I said. "What should I do?"

"You've got to tell Mrs. Bacon," Ryan said.

I raised my hand.

"Is something wrong, A.J.?" Mrs. Bacon asked.

"I . . . uh . . . just had a bathroom emergency," I told her.

"Oh, dear," said Mrs. Bacon. "Should I call the nurse?"

"You'd better call the custodian," said Ryan.

That's when the weirdest thing in the history of the world happened. You'll never believe who came into room 303 at that moment.

It was our custodian, Miss Lazar! She was riding an electric scooter and carrying a toilet bowl plunger.

Miss Lazar is like a real superhero. Anytime something goes wrong, she saves the day. She can clean up any mess and fix anything that breaks. She's the only one in the school who can turn on the lights in the all-porpoise room because she has a special key.

"It is I, Super Custodian!" Miss Lazar announced. "Any time somebody loses a retainer in the garbage can, or a student throws up in the cafeteria, I'm at your service. What happened?"

"There seems to be a situation in the boys' bathroom," Mrs. Bacon told her.

"A situation?" said Miss Lazar. "I *love* situations! You can count on me!"

She scooted down the hall to the boys' room.

I followed her, telling her exactly what happened. When we got to the bathroom, she took a yellow rubber glove out of her pocket and put it on.

"I'm really sorry," I told Miss Lazar as she stuck her hand into the toilet bowl.

"No worries," she said cheerfully as she fished around in there. "I *love* it when kids drop things into toilet bowls. If kids didn't drop things into toilet bowls, I wouldn't have a job. In fact, I wish kids would drop *more* things into toilet bowls."

Miss Lazar is bizarre.

"Got it!" she said, pulling out my mouthpiece. We washed it off in the sink.

"It's clean as a whistle," she said, which

makes no sense at all because whistles are full of spit too.

When we got back to room 303, I told everybody what happened.

"Hooray for Miss Lazar!" everybody shouted. She hopped back on her scooter.

"It's all in a day's work," she said. "Well, I have to go mop up the cafeteria. Duty calls!" Then she scooted out of the room.

We all giggled because Miss Lazar said "duty," which sounds just like "doody." It's okay to say "duty," but we're not supposed to say "doody." Nobody knows why. If you ask me, those things should have different-sounding words.

When class was over, Mrs. Bacon pulled me aside.

"A.J.," she said, "you didn't have to go to the bathroom to empty your spit valve."

"I didn't?"

"Of course not," she told me. "Professional musicians don't go to the bathroom every time they have to empty their spit valve."

"What do they do?" I asked.

"They just empty it on the floor," said Mrs. Bacon.

Ugh, disgusting! Professional musicians are gross!

Feeling the Buns

Practice makes perfect. That's what Mrs. Bacon tells us.

When I got home from school, I could have practiced playing my tuba, but I decided to play video games instead. Then I was going to practice my tuba after dinner, but there was a game on TV, so I watched it. Then I was going to practice my tuba after the game was over, but I had to clean my room because my mom told me to do that about a year ago. Then I was going to practice my tuba after I cleaned my room, but it was almost bedtime, so it was too late to practice my tuba.

All week long, I had a lot of important stuff to do that made it impossible to practice my tuba. I had to make my bed. I had to floss my teeth. I had to line up my collection of Pez dispensers in size order. You know, important stuff.

When I got to school the next Thursday, there were sixteen geese out in the playground. *Sixteen!* I counted them. They were multiplying. I didn't even know geese could do math!

That's a joke. But seriously, not only were the geese multiplying, they were also dropping their goose poop all over the playground. It was gross.

After we pledged the allegiance, we went to room 303.

"Have you kids been practicing?" Mrs. Bacon asked as we walked in.

"I forgot," said Michael.

"I forgot," said Alexia.

"I forgot," said Ryan.

"I forgot," said Neil.

"I forgot," said Emily.

Mrs. Bacon didn't look happy.

"*I've* been practicing!" shouted Andrea. Ugh.

"Okay," Mrs. Bacon said, "let's try 'Hot Cross Buns.'"

I sat between Ryan and Little Miss Perfect. Mrs. Bacon waved her chopstick around and we played "Hot Cross Buns." It sounded horrible.

"No!" shouted Mrs. Bacon. "You're not *feeling* the buns!"

After we finished the song, Andrea leaned over to me.

"Hey, Arlo," she whispered. "Can you play solo?"

"Sure," I said.

"Then why don't you play so low we can't hear you?"

"Oh, snap!" said Ryan.

Playing tuba is *hard*. You've got to push those buttons and blow into the mouthpiece and hold the big tuba up all at the same time. But Mrs. Bacon said I was making progress, and she gave me my yellow belt. Of course, Little Miss Know-It-All had already earned her yellow, orange, green, and blue belts. Why can't a truck full of hot cross buns fall on her head?

After we played the song a few more times, Mrs. Bacon taught us a song with four notes—"Mary Had a Little Lamb." That's a weird song. It's about a lamb that follows a girl to school. Why would a lamb go to school? If I was a lamb, I would just stand around eating grass all day. School is the *last* place I'd go.

Besides, how would a barnyard animal get through school security? At my school, visitors can't come in unless they show their ID to Officer Spence, our security guard. If a lamb ever snuck into our school, there would be a lockdown, and Officer Spence would probably shoot it with a tranquilizer dart.

Anyway, after we learned "Mary Had a Little Lamb," Mrs. Bacon taught us some other songs that don't have many notes in them: "Row, Row, Row Your Boat," "The Itsy Bitsy Spider," "The Wheels on the Bus," and "Bohemian Rhapsody." She said we would play all those songs at our big recital. It was only two weeks away.*

You know what? I have to admit it. By

_____

*What's brown and sits on a piano bench?
Beethoven's last movement.

the end of the class, our little band was actually getting pretty good. You could almost tell what song we were playing without being told the name of it.

When we left the band room that day, Mrs. Bacon pulled me aside. She said I was doing a great job on the tuba, and she gave me *another* belt, the orange one.

It was the greatest day of my life.

Big Gig

When I got to school the next Thursday, all the geese were gone from the playground. That was weird. Where did they go? Back to Canada, I guess.

"Big news, kids!" said Mrs. Bacon when we got to room 303. "We have our first gig this morning!"

When a group of musicians play in front of people, it's called a "gig." Nobody knows why.

"I'm scared," said Emily, who's scared of everything.

"There's no need to be nervous," said Mrs. Bacon. "This is just a warm-up for our recital next week. Grab your instruments and Pringle up!"

We walked a million hundred miles to the front of the school, where the bus was waiting.

"Bingle boo!" said Mrs. Kormel, our bus driver.

That means "hello" in her secret language. Mrs. Kormel is not normal.

We drove a million hundred minutes

until we reached a big building. The sign on the front said SHADY REST SENIOR HOME.

"We're going to play for senior citizens?" Michael asked as we piled out of the bus.

"Yes!" said Mrs. Bacon. "But not just *any* senior citizens."

And you'll never believe who came out of Shady Rest Senior Home to greet us.

It was Ella Mentry, the lady our school was named after! She must live there. Mrs. Mentry was a teacher at our school a long time ago.

"I'm happy to welcome you kids to Shady Rest," said Mrs. Mentry. "My friends and I can't wait to hear you play."

We walked inside. Mrs. Mentry led us

to a big room with bleachers. We climbed
up on the bleachers and unpacked our
instruments. The senior citizens came
into the room and sat in chairs. Some of
them were already sitting in wheelchairs.

Mrs. Mentry stood up and all the senior
citizens clapped.

"My friends," she announced. "I'm

proud to introduce you to some wonderful students who attend the school that
was named after me. These third graders
would like to serenade you. This is their
first concert ever."

"Woo-hooo!" some old guy shouted.
"Rock and roll!"

"'Stairway to Heaven'!" somebody
shouted.

"Pink Floyd!"

"'Free Bird'!"

I had no idea what they were shouting
about. Mrs. Bacon waved her chopstick,
and we started playing "Hot Cross Buns."
We were all a little nervous, but if you ask
me, we *crushed* it.

The senior citizens gave us a nice round

of applause. I think they would have given us a standing ovation, but a lot of them couldn't stand up.

"AC/DC!" shouted an old lady.

"More cowbell!"

Mrs. Bacon waved her chopstick, and we played "Mary Had a Little Lamb." Again, we were awesome.* While the senior citi-

---

*Why can't skeletons play in church?
They have no organs.

zens were cheering and clapping, Mrs. Bacon gathered us around her.

"Okay," she whispered, "clean out your spit valves."

"Where?" I asked.

"On the bleachers," she replied.

Gross! But who was I to argue? We emptied our spit valves on the bleachers. And you'll never believe who walked through the door at that moment.

Nobody! Doors are made of wood. You can't walk through a piece of wood! When are you gonna learn? But you'll never believe who opened the door and came into the room.

It was Dr. Carbles, the president of the

Board of Education! He walked in just as I was blowing a load of spit out of my tuba.

Mrs. Bacon waved her chopstick, and we started playing "The Itsy Bitsy Spider." That's when the weirdest thing in the history of the world happened.

Emily must have slipped on some spit because she stumbled a little. The end of her flute poked into the back of Alexia's head!

Alexia screamed, and the slide part of her trombone went flying!

It got caught in Andrea's hair! She freaked out and bumped into me!

I lost my balance, and my tuba slammed into Ryan!

His French horn fell on Michael's foot!

Michael hopped up and banged into Neil, and then everybody fell off the bleachers, even Mrs. Bacon!

The next thing we knew, all of us were tangled up in a big heap on the floor! Arms and legs and instruments were everywhere! Everybody was yelling and screaming and hooting and hollering and freaking out. Alexia's trombone slide was wrapped around Ryan's neck. Mrs. Bacon's head was poking through Neil's drum. You should have *been* there! It was ridorkulous!

While all this was happening, Dr. Carbles stood there looking really angry.

The senior citizens clapped, but that

was the end of our gig. We packed up our instruments and left the Shady Rest Senior Home.

As we were walking out the door, a lady handed me a note. It said, "Thank you for coming to play for us. I thought your music was wonderful!"

I showed it to Mrs. Bacon and asked her why the lady wrote a note instead of just telling us she liked our music.

"She was asleep the whole time," Mrs. Bacon told me. "She didn't hear a note you played."

Spelling Counts

We climbed back onto the bus. Mrs. Bacon sat in the first row by herself. A few minutes later, I heard strange sounds coming from her seat. That's when I realized she was crying.

I didn't think Mrs. Bacon was fakin'.

We all went to the front of the bus to give her hugs and tissues. That's what you do when somebody's crying.

"What's the matter, Mrs. Bacon?" asked Emily.

Mrs. Bacon wiped her face.

"I'm a big failure," she whimpered. "The recital next week is going to be a disaster.

I don't know what to do. You kids aren't ready. I only have a half an hour a week to teach you how to play all the songs. It's not enough time. You're not practicing at home. I'm stressed out. Dr. Carbles is going to fire me, and nobody will ever hire me again. My career is over."

Then she started crying again.

"Don't worry, Mrs. Bacon," said Andrea. "Everything is going to be okay."

"We're going to put on a *great* show at the recital," said Alexia.

"Yeah," I added. "We're going to make you proud of us. We're going to practice really hard."

And we did. We practiced like crazy

all week. I didn't waste my time playing video games or lining up my Pez dispensers. All I did was practice playing tuba. I played "Hot Cross Buns" so many times, I was really beginning to *feel* the buns.*

Finally, the day of our big recital arrived. I had to wear a tie to school. Ugh! A sign in the front said we should walk around to the playground. There were a bunch of chairs set up out there, and lots of grown-ups—Mrs. Bacon, Mr. Klutz, Mr. Cooper, Mr. Loring. Dr. Carbles was there too, with his mean face.

"It's such a beautiful day," said Mrs.

---

*What kind of music are balloons afraid of?
Pop music.

Bacon, "I thought it would be nice to have the recital outdoors. I'm going to pass out—"

"She's gonna pass out!" I yelled. "Give her air!"

"I'm going to pass out programs," continued Mrs. Bacon. "I made them myself."

Mrs. Bacon handed everybody one of her programs.

People were ushered to their seats by the PTA. That stands for "Parents who talk a lot." Ryan's mom, Mrs. Dole, is president of the PTA. She was carrying a big platter.

"Guess what I made?" she said.

"What?" everybody asked.

"Hot cross buns!" said Mrs. Dole.

She passed out buns to the audience, but we couldn't eat any yet because it was time to take our places on the stage. Bummer in the summer!

"Are you nervous?" Ryan asked me as he picked up his French horn.

"Yeah."

We were all on pins and needles.

Well, not really. We were sitting on chairs. If we were on pins and needles, it would have hurt. But there was electricity in the air.

Well, not really. If there was electricity in the air, we would get electrocuted.

Mr. Klutz held up his hand and made a peace sign, which means shut up.

"Welcome to the third-grade recital," he announced. "The students have been working very hard on their music, and they're excited to play for you today. Ready, kids?"

Mrs. Bacon raised her chopstick, and we played "Hot Cross Buns." It was great.

After that, we played "Mary Had a Little Lamb." It was awesome. We didn't miss a note. The parents were all smiling and clapping for us. It was the greatest day of my life.

We took a minute to empty our spit valves. It was time to play "The Itsy Bitsy

Spider." That's when the weirdest thing in the history of the world happened. I heard a noise in the distance.

"Do you hear something?" I whispered to Neil.

"Yeah, what is it?" he whispered back.

"Beats me," I whispered.

The noise was getting louder. And *closer*.

"What is that annoying sound?" asked Mrs. Bacon.

"Look! Up in the sky!" shouted Ryan.

I looked up.

"It's a bird!" shouted Michael.

"No, it's a *bunch* of birds!" shouted Alexia.

And that's when I realized IT WAS THE GEESE! They were coming back! There were dozens of them flying in a big V shape, honking and squawking like crazy!

"They're heading this way!" shouted Andrea.

She was right. The birds were coming right at us! I saw it with my own eyes!

Well, it would be pretty hard to see something with somebody else's eyes.

"We've got to *do* something!" shouted Emily.

"Help!" somebody screamed.

"The geese are attacking!" I shouted.

"No, they're not!" shouted Andrea. "That's their mating call! They must have heard us playing and they fell in love with our instruments!"

"Run for your lives!" shouted Neil.

The next thing we knew, the geese were dive-bombing and landing all around us.

"A bird pooped on my flute!" shouted Emily.

"Help!" I shouted. "I think a goose is in love with my tuba!"

"The geese are eating my hot cross buns!" shouted Mrs. Dole. "Protect the buns!"

Mrs. Dole was out of control!

Everybody was yelling and screaming and hooting and hollering and freaking out. Emily slipped on some spit and fell off the stage. Parents were jumping off their chairs. It was ridorkulous!

Mr. Klutz hollered for us to get into the school right away. After everyone was safely inside, Dr. Carbles slammed the door so the geese couldn't follow us. He looked *really* mad.

"That's the last straw!" he shouted at Mrs. Bacon. "You're fired!"

One-Woman Band

10

What did straws have to do with any-thing? And why are grown-ups always running out of them? Can't they just buy a new box of straws before the old box is empty?

It was really sad that Mrs. Bacon got

102

fired. It made for a sad ending to this story. But hey, who decided that stories have to have a happy ending, anyway?

Actually, the next day the weirdest thing in the history of the world happened. The guys and I were going to get ice-cream cones after school when we saw Mrs. Bacon standing on the corner all by herself. She had a drum strapped to her back, a trumpet and a kazoo in front of her face, a cymbal on her head, a tambourine on her knee, and a violin in her hands. Oh, and she had the biggest smile on her face. And you'll never believe what song she was playing.

"Hot Cross Buns"!*

Well, that's pretty much what happened.
Maybe Mrs. Bacon will get her job back.

---

*Why do bagpipers walk while they play?
They're trying to get away from the music.

Maybe I'll earn my black belt. Maybe they'll have music on Uranus. Maybe I'll play the tuba with my ears. Maybe musicians will stop emptying their spit valves all over the floor. Maybe Officer Spence will shoot that lamb with a tranquilizer dart. Maybe Mrs. Bacon will go get Chinese food. Maybe I can talk somebody into putting ridorkulous in the dictionary.

But it won't be easy!

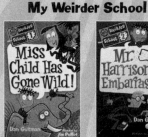